CW00865352

Short Stories

For Older, and Not Quite So Old, Children

by

Dandi Palmer

Dodo Books

Copyright Dandi Palmer 2010

These stories are works of fiction and any resemblance
to persons living or dead is purely coincidental.

ISBN   978 1 906442 25 5

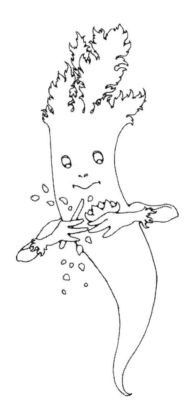

<u>Stories</u>

Abbess Honoria
Honour the past, or pay the price

Custard Doughnuts
Confectionary and stone carving

Dream Fungus
A friend from another dimension

The Ghosts of the Greasy Spoon
Haunted junk food

Hot Chocolate
Never trust a four-year-old's grasp of arithmetic

The Jugle Egg
How to hatch a new Universe

The Odd Fish
A chatty fossil

Queenie
Rodent with the ultimate weapon in its paws

Sammy's Sandwich
Strange snacks for a strange friend

Tigger, Treacle, and Coke
Friendship knows no boundaries

Twillington's Tip
Where rubbish goes

Zalda Zax and the Cyberpod
Flight of fancy into a different dimension

ABBESS HONORIA

Written before the UK Hunting Act 2004 was passed

Several dozen hooves crunched over the frosted ground. Some distance ahead hounds bayed as they followed the scent of the fox.

Suddenly there was silence, and then whimpering as the beagles turned tail and fled back along the track, through the hooves of the horses.

"Hunt saboteurs!" bellowed the master of the hunt. This was unlikely as he had managed to get the protesters' ringleaders jailed for criminal trespass weeks ago. But he was in a fury and spurred his horse forward to give any interloper the taste of his riding crop.

Before they could catch up, the rest of the hunt heard an indignant whinny, terrified yell, and dull thud as sixteen stone of retired bank manager hit the frozen ground.

There was a ghostly figure blocking their way. By its flowing white robe it might have been some Glastonbury hippy on a quest to find the Holy Grail.

The hunt closed in. There was no one else watching, so they could get away with giving the trespasser a good hiding. However, when they could see beyond their cloud of anger, it transpired that the interloper was a tall, elderly woman wearing the robes of some religious order. She was surrounded by an eerie halo. All the same, she was trespassing: there was only one way to deal with poachers and trespassers. The hunt might well have trampled the holy woman into the ground if she had not raised her hands and formed a shimmering arch in the cold air.

More horses panicked and unseated their riders.

The arch filled with light that crackled and spat like a living creature.

Terrified horses and bruised hunters fled.

The apparition faded and a lucky fox continued on its round of the local rabbit warrens.

On the hill above, despite the barking of dogs and whinnying of horses, Gillian ignored the commotion. She had seen it all before and was more interested in wrapping her remaining sandwich, putting on her mittens, and climbing down from her perch on the crumbling monastery wall.

Somebody was walking through the ancient tombstones in the graveyard with a businesslike stride. The woman had a large key in her hand and was heading towards the crypt - she must have been going to open it!

Gillian knew she wouldn't get a chance like this again. That crypt had been out of bounds to visitors for years and the woman with the two wave radio chattering somewhere inside her quilted jacket was obviously going inside.

Gillian tried to appear casual as she strolled past her line of sight, peering intently at the inscriptions on each gravestone and jotting down the odd note in her pad.

The woman had an air of officialdom about her and looked at the 10-year-old as though she were at risk of becoming lunch for the peregrine circling high above them. "Hello."

Gillian was used to adults looking at her as though she was out of place. "Hello," she replied with an engaging smile.

"Are you up here all by yourself?" There was a schoolmarmish authority in those firm tones.

"It's alright." Gillian pulled a mobile phone from her pocket. "I only live in the estate down there and have to check in every hour, and Harry always comes as soon as I call."

"Harry?"

"Our Alsatian."

"He's got a mobile phone?"

"No ... I didn't mean ..."

The woman laughed and the sternness evaporated. "It's alright. I know what you meant."

Gillian couldn't contain her curiosity any longer. "Are you going into the crypt?"

"That's why I've got the key."

"They don't let anyone in there as a rule - that's what the museum curator told me."

"I've got special permission. One of the perks of my job."

"Who are you then?"

"Detective Sergeant Jardine."

Gillian's face lit up. "Police! Are you investigating the white lady?"

DS Jardine looked puzzled. "What white lady?"

"The one that leaves the crypt every time there's a hunt."

The detective looked at the iron gate securing the crypt, then at Gillian. "Tell me about her?"

"Let me come inside with you then?"

The 10-year-old looked and sounded mature for her years, and obviously had a keen interest in local knowledge which might be useful.

DS Jardine unlocked the gate and took out her torch, beckoning Gillian after her.

They went down a dark passage and into the crypt where there was enough light coming through the gratings high in the outside wall to see without the torch.

Gillian enthusiastically examined every tomb and inscription. If the police officer wanted to find a body here, she was spoilt for choice.

"What are you looking for?"

"I'm not sure. We had to bring charges against the hunt saboteurs for criminal trespass and some were sent to prison. But their leader claimed that the land had been bequeathed by the Abbess, 'For the good and well being of God's creatures and the people.' So I decided to check on the story just to confirm that those who claim the land actually have title to it."

"And?" Gillian asked as innocently as she could.

"The ancestral owners allowed us to examine the deeds... However..."

"They were a forgery?"

"If so, a very good one. The key document doesn't mention Abbess Honoria."

4

"So those protesters could be set free if you find her will?"

"If only it were that simple. If a court decides that the people do own the land and ruins, they will probably end up with the National trust." DSI Jardine paused to wonder why she was telling the 10-year-old all this. For some reason it didn't seem to matter, so she went on. "But that's not why I'm here. If this land doesn't belong to the current owner, a multi-million pound fraud is about to be perpetrated."

"Why?"

"Leaving it to the moles and rabbits didn't matter before, but this land has now become very valuable to speculators; valuable enough to make it worthwhile forging a few ancient documents."

"Wow! You shouldn't really have told me all that, should you?"

DS Jardine was baffled that she had. The police officer had the reputation of being tight lipped in the most stressful of situations. "Not really." She brushed some grime from an inscription, none the wiser about what she was looking for. "Now Gillian, tell me about the lady in white?"

"She's in here now," the 10-year-old announced brightly.

"In here..?" The detective tried not to shudder at the strange change in her young companion and the crypt's air pressure. "How can you tell?"

"Look." Gillian pointed to a tall white shape forming in the gloom at the far end of the crypt.

The apparition wore a robe that fluttered eerily in the still icy air and the only features visible were the long severe face and a hand pointing to a skull in a niche.

Undaunted, Gillian skipped over to lift it down. "It's very heavy for bone."

The figure in white immediately became a ghostly whirlwind.

Before Gillian could hand the skull to DS Jardine it whirled from her grasp and shattered on the flagstones.

The detective trained her torch on the remains. "Good grief, it was clay."

Gillian pulled a large iron key from the shards. "This must open her coffin."

"But Abbess Honoria's remains are in a casket in the cathedral."

"Well let's go before anyone realises we've discovered the key."

"Now hold on ..."

"The white lady will only let me open it, you know," Gillian announced confidently.

The detective had no doubt about that, then an anxious Alsatian looking for its 10-year-old owner pattered down the crypt passage, so she decided to let the strange girl hold onto the key.

Once Harry was taken back home and Gillian's parents were satisfied that she was in safe hands, DS Jardine drove her and the key to the cathedral.

Clutching a can of WD-40, the deaconess led Gillian, DS Jardine, a forensic scientist, and party of interested clerics down into the cathedral crypt. "It's such a heavy lock. Even the recent burglars couldn't get into the casket; they just scratched the wood. No idea why they thought there would have been anything of value in it? Only an acetylene torch could cut through those iron bands, and that would have set off the sprinklers."

The deaconess and other clerics seemed unaware that they were caretakers of the evidence that could foil a multi-million pound fraud.

As the party reached the massive steel and wood casket, the deaconess turned to Gillian. "You do know they'll be bones, hair, and such like ... in there?"

"Oh those things won't bother her," said DS Jardine. "After all these centuries, I'll just be surprised if she can turn that key."

The deaconess sprayed the inside of the lock with WD-40 and Gillian pushed the key home. As she carefully turned it there was a 'clunk' and a sudden gush of the air was released from the lid.

A faint, eerie sigh echoed through the crypt columns.

The forensic scientist lifted the lid of the casket. Inside it was a jumble of human bones in a decaying white robe. Skeleton hands clutched a manuscript box. He flicked away the dust of centuries with a soft brush, and then the deaconess put on her spectacles to translate the Latin inscription on its lid.

"This is the will of Abbess Honoria, witnessed by God and her holy order."

She looked up. "Seems as though the legend might have been true after all."

"Legend? What legend?" asked DS Jardine.

"Didn't you know? Nobody could prove it because her mortal remains could not be disturbed on pain of death, but it was believed the King tried to take her lands for the royal hunt. So she left her estate to the holy order, God's animals and the common people ... on condition no one ever hunted on it."

CUSTARD DOUGHNUTS

Sadie liked custard doughnuts. Strawberry, raspberry and even chocolate fillings were great, but nothing could beat that smooth, sweet taste of custard and pastry that filled you with a glowing sensation.

Sadie had tried custard tarts, and custard with apple pie or treacle pudding. Somehow it wasn't the same. While all her school friends queued for crisps, coke and chocolate bars, Sadie preferred to walk to the patisserie and collect her custard doughnut.

Apart from her daughter's expanding waistline, Sadie's mother was also worried that this pastry preference was becoming the highlight of a young life that should have been filled with pop videos, parties, and boys.

So Sadie's parents upgraded her computer, paid some computer geek to write a program that blocked pornography websites - and any reference to custard doughnuts - in the hope she would spend her spare time surfing the Web instead of pursuing confectionery.

Sadie took to the Internet like a wart hog to mud. She wallowed in the online art galleries, interactive discussions on the state of the planet, and simulations of sounds made by dinosaurs.

But, most importantly, she Googled custard doughnuts. It came up with caramel doughnuts, iced doughnuts, dinky doughnuts, even doughnuts for dogs - but no custard doughnuts. Sadie was puzzled. How was it possible that such a comprehensive search engine couldn't find anything about custard doughnuts? Then she started to believe that they had been a figment of her imagination and it was just fate that she lived near the only patisserie on the planet that made them.

One night Sadie went to bed sadly perplexed over the matter and woke the next morning feeling as though a void had opened up in her life. It wasn't until lunch time that she realised what had happened - her craving for custard doughnuts had disappeared.

As time passed, that void demanded to be filled, yet it seemed that nothing could compensate for Sadie's old pastry addiction. Sport may have been all right, but she was too big and clumsy to pirouette on the asymmetrical bars. Reading was fine if you could find something that didn't involve fluffy animals or teenage angst, and there were only so many times you could play video games before everything became a blur. So Sadie sat in her bedroom, immersed in the Internet.

Downstairs, her parents congratulated themselves that they had weaned their daughter away from her old craving for deep fried pastry which exuded a gelatinous yellow mixture. Perhaps she would now find a nice online club that wanted to save the whale, or even take cyber hikes across the Himalayas.

Weeks passed. Sadie's friends occasionally called to go with her to the school's disco club. Her parents held their breath. Perhaps their big, clumsy, daughter was developing into a well balanced young woman after all.

Then, in the middle of summer, a truck pulled up outside the house. It was carrying large blocks of stone.

Sadie's mother looked aghast at the delivery slip. 'One 70x40x30cm of rough sawn limestone. Cost & delivery PAID.' She had no choice but to allow the two delivery men to wheel it into the back garden where it sat by the patio as though a gigantic garden gnome wanted to burst from it.

Before going to her morning coffee club, Sadie's mother went up to her daughter's room. Under the bed she found a wooden box containing three stone chisels, a file, rasp, dust mask, protective goggles and a three pound iron hammer. It was now apparent what Sadie had done with all the money she had saved by not buying custard doughnuts.

Sadie's first efforts with the hammer and chisel produced something shaped like an amoeba. It might have been useful as a giant's doorstop, and provoked several enquiries from neighbours anxious that the council had commissioned some modern sculpture to offend local taste. With help from the stone carver's website she had discovered, Sadie's work quickly improved.

As her father looked out over his flower beds punctuated by huge stone animals, he wondered if he didn't after all prefer a plump, custard doughnut loving daughter instead of one with arms like Popeye capable of flattening the neighbourhood bullies. At least his golfing friends were impressed and their club commissioned Sadie to carve something monolithic as an interesting hazard on the ninth hole. It may have been paranoia, but when the sculpture was finished, her father had the horrible suspicion that it looked like a gigantic custard doughnut.

DREAM FUNGUS

Published by Aquila in September 1994

It was still there, tucked secretively away amongst the nettle stems like an abandoned ostrich egg. Lee decided to tell no one about the puffball, even though it was safe from his father's strimmer. His mother insisted the bottom of the garden be kept for the butterflies, and any other wild creatures that could make it through the nettles.

Over the next few days the puffball rapidly grew. Lee was tall for his ten years, but it was soon up to his waist. The books said that these fungi could become very large, but Lee wanted to know what happened when they finished growing. This one surely couldn't get any larger and he had the feeling that when he came out the next morning he would find a collapsed brown shell.

Lee just told his parents that he wanted to camp out all night to watch a shower of meteors. As it was the weekend, his parents agreed on condition that Damien, their black Labrador stay with him. Having a large dog bounce on your head in the dead of night was bad enough, but the thought of suddenly encountering its wet nose in the early hours at the

11

bottom of the garden almost persuaded Lee to cancel the adventure. But his father had already put up the tent and was making him a plate of cheese and radish sandwiches, so there was no way out.

As darkness fell Lee was not sure what to expect. After pulling back several nettles, he slipped into his sleeping bag to watch from the tent as the puffball shone in the moonlight. Hedgehogs crunched their way round it and the occasional frog flopped near Damien's nose. When one croaked the Labrador hid in the nearest bush.

"Fine guard dog you are," muttered Lee, and then dozed off.

When he woke the moon was high and the puffball even larger than ever, glowing now as though it had a lamp inside it. Lee rubbed his eyes and sat up. The fungus seemed to be hollow. The skin of the smooth sphere was now patterned like a stained glass window and, gradually, the surrounding nettles, bushes and the tent were spangled with luminous colour.

Lee became alarmed, but Damien was nowhere to be seen. That dog had got cowardice down to a fine art. But this was no time to run and wake your parents. Something incredible was about to happen, so why waste time telling people who wouldn't appreciate it?

Something else was going on. As Lee got to his feet... he walked right through the tent. He was no longer standing quite on the ground and felt even less happy about this when he turned to see himself still fast asleep just inside the tent. Perhaps it was time to go back? If only he knew how.

Inside the giant puffball a shape was forming. The kaleidoscope colours cleared to reveal a small figure seated inside the sphere. Balanced on its lap was another sphere about the size of an orange surrounded by a bright halo of light. Two webbed, three-fingered hands enclosed the small sphere and the light dimmed so Lee could clearly see the creature holding it. The head was elegantly domed, covered in neat silver curls and the torso short and sturdy, dressed neck to ankle in a rippling diaphanous robe. At first there didn't seem to be any feet - but as the alien rose it appeared to be standing on points, rather like the ballerinas Lee's great grandmother drew. The creature was so like her pictures she must have seen it as well. That was one of the reasons the family had her put in a home; that and breaking the speed limit whenever she managed to get her hands on some car keys.

Apart from standing up, the creature in the puffball remained still, watching the ten-year-old as though coming to a decision. "Who are you?" Lee eventually asked, a little disconcerted by the penetrating gaze of its deep mauve eyes.

"I'm sorry if I disturbed you," it said in perfect English.

"It's alright. If I hadn't woken up I would have got a crick in my neck anyway."

"But you haven't woken up."

Lee looked back down at his slumbering body. "No, I haven't, have I?"

"You wouldn't be able to see me if you were awake."

"Why not?"

"I can only travel in other people's dreams."

Lee was puzzled. "I don't get it."

"You understand that distance is a dimension?"

"Yes."

"Time is a dimension?"

"I...think I do."

"So are dreams." The alien lifted the small sphere. "This is my ship. It takes me into the most convenient shell available. When I visited your ancestor I always used to appear in the mirror on the dressing table."

"Used to?"

"It has been removed for some reason. There is no other furniture through which I can communicate."

"I think the mirror was broken. Great gran was taking practice putts in her bedroom." Lee pondered. "Will any mirror do?"

"The larger the better."

"OK then." The alien started to fade. "Hey! Just a minute."

"What is it?"

"How do you do that? ... I mean will I ever see you again?"

"Oh yes," smiled the alien, "when you reach 80."

And the apparition faded.

Lee woke next morning with a crick in his neck and the spores of a giant puffball all over the tent, himself, Damien and the cheese and radish sandwiches.

Lee had never seen the point in having two mirrors in his room. They did help you look into infinity, but he suspected that the one screwed to the wardrobe door was a device to remind him in duplicate that his room needed tidying up. He persuaded his mother that the spare mirror would be better screwed to the front of the wardrobe door in his great gran's room in the home.

Lee's mother was surprised at the old lady's reaction. The occasional pot plant had never received the same appreciation. Perhaps it had something to do with the small picture of the alien Lee had taped to a corner of the mirror.

THE GHOSTS OF THE GREASY SPOON

Deepa led her dog, Bengi, over the footbridge and down to the deserted roadside café. It had been closed ever since the bypass opened; now only the occasional cyclist passed this way.

A sign still swung in the breeze on its one remaining hinge. Its faded words declared defiantly, "Burgers, Fries, and Full English Breakfasts". It sounded very greasy.

Deepa pushed the door and, to her surprise, it swung open. She apprehensively looked about and couldn't believe what she saw. The interior was immaculate, considering how long it had been closed. Chairs were neatly arranged at tables with scrubbed plastic tablecloths on which condiments sat in strict formation, and the counter's teaspoons gleamed on the ends of their chains.

Deepa stepped inside. Bengi whimpered apprehensively. He might have remembered that dogs weren't allowed in cafés, or perhaps something else was bothering him? Deepa was too intrigued to wonder what it was. The café should have been derelict.

Bengi refused to follow her in and remained on the doormat, shivering.

Deepa confidently went to the counter and would have bought a packet of crisps if there had been anyone about.

Out of the corner of her eye she glimpsed something sitting cross legged on the juke box. When she turned it had gone.

By the counter were some swing doors that must have led somewhere. Deepa pushed them open and walked through. Filling one wall of the huge kitchen was a cooking range. It had been blackened with years of burnt fat and the occasional uncontrolled fire.

Then Deepa realised why Bengi had stayed outside shivering.

Hovering over the scene of a thousand culinary disasters was a dense smudge the size of a duvet. It had arms, a tapering tail, and face with a wide greasy grin. The harder Deepa stared, the more solid it became.

A white table with a vase of flowers looked very out of place in this hell's kitchen. The contrast with the blackened cooking range was so striking, Deepa didn't immediately see the slender, airy shape sitting beside it. Too tall to be a fairy, this entity had an aura of celery about it and wore a wistful expression, like a flower that needed watering.

Deepa turned to run out of the kitchen. The greasy smudge snatched up a huge iron frying pan and blocked her way.

"A customer! A customer!"

Deepa was alarmed. Ghosts weren't meant to recognise the living, let alone threaten to cook for them. "Well - I wasn't stopping - actually."

The smudge wasn't going to allow the interloper to escape that easily and hovered closer. "But you must!"

"I only have enough money for a packet of crisps."

"You're the first customer we've had for years! We wouldn't dream of making you pay!"

Deepa thought fast. "Anyway, I'm a vegetarian."

This dampened the greasy smudge's enthusiasm and, obviously offended, it backed off a little.

Deepa recovered her curiosity. "This place has been closed for years. I remember the last owners leaving. Who are you?"

"Me? I'm the ghost of a million burnt burgers." The greasy smudge spun on its tail and flourished the frying pan in the direction of the white table. "And there sits the spirit of side salad."

"And what was that creature I saw crouching on the juke box?"

The two ghosts glanced at each other apprehensively.

"Oh that creature," moaned the spirit of side salad. "I'd rather you didn't mention it."

The smudge gave an evil chuckle. "Daren't sit in the same room - those two."

"Well who is it then?" insisted Deepa.

"He's the cholesterol goblin."

The spirit of side salad floated from its seat. "Well, as you're a vegetarian, what could be better than a nice salad?"

"With chips," insisted the greasy smudge. "And I know I have some vegeburgers somewhere about." The smudge threw open a freezer's lid and rummaged through its contents like a whirlwind.

"No, really," protested Deepa. "I'll have a meal when I get back - and I said I wouldn't be long."

The smudge tossed a large bag of frozen chips and a catering size box of strange coloured burgers into a deep fryer full of boiling fat. "Won't take a minute!"

Hot oil spattered the walls and grated carrot flew as the two cooks attempted to outdo each other.

"Will you be more careful!" chided the spirit of side salad as it chopped cucumber and made fancy flowers with radishes.

Between them the ghosts were preparing enough food to feed a convention of lapsed dieters. There was no way they were going to get that meal onto one plate.

The greasy smudge tossed the chips and burgers in the hot oil as though it was flipping pancakes.

"You'll start a fire!" Deepa warned.

"Fire!" laughed the smudge. "Used to have them all the time. Happy days!"

No sooner were the words out of its wide greasy mouth than the deep fryer slipped from its nebulous fingers. The contents fell onto a red hot element of the cooker and a ball of flame hit the ceiling.

Deepa ran for her life, back out through the swing doors into the cafe.

The round, wicked looking cholesterol goblin was sitting cross legged on the counter, shrieking with laughter.

"No insurance! No insurance!" Then it rolled onto the floor and bounced up and down like a yo-yo.

Deepa seized Bengi's lead and they ran. Neither dared to look back until they reached the safety of the footbridge,

A column of smoke and fire was billowing into the sky.

The fire service answered her emergency call in minutes, though by the time they arrived there was nothing left of the café. As it was due to be demolished, not many questions were asked about the cause of the fire.

Despite what had happened, Deepa knew that its odd occupants were still out there, in some other cafe, boosting the nation's cholesterol level.

HOT CHOCOLATE

Suki had at last gathered enough slivers of rock to put into her mineral analyser. The other fossil hunters thought she was wasting her time on the thin dark strata: the tar deposits their dentists frequently removed from their molars would have produced better samples.

Suki fed in the crumbs of rock. The mineral analyser's display blinked as though baffled. Several minutes passed before the machine reluctantly admitted its conclusion. Suki's thin rock seam had been formed 65 million years ago from a sea of chocolate - with traces of hazelnut. Did dinosaurs not only browse on cycads and devour meat running with warm blood, but have a sweet tooth as well? Suki doubted it. Her mineral analyser must have developed an embarrassing glitch, which she daren't let the other part-time palaeontologists know about, so she discreetly left as they chipped away at their own allocated fossil beds.

Suki also decided not to declare her unlikely find to the party's organisers before she had checked that a sea of chocolate had not really flooded the late Cretaceous continent.

Technology was a wonderful thing; with it you could count the grains of sand in your favourite holiday desert, or calculate the chemical composition of your current pimple. There were also amazing travel cubicles that could take you to any time or place like magic carpets - even fly you over the minarets of ancient Baghdad.

Suki was old enough to realise that these excursions were only illusion, however real the holographic technicians made them seem. All the same, because the Cretaceous era of 65 million years ago was filled with fierce creatures, Suki had

20

to use her palaeontologist's permit to enter the cubicle programmed for that period. Some travellers had been pulled out of them gibbering about aliens, dragons, and gullies running with gore. The shock of seeing another reality was often too great for the modern mind to cope with and many of them didn't totally recover. A permit was meant to guarantee that its owner's mind was too well-balanced to be unhinged.

Though it had never happened, the technicians were aware that if there was a powerful enough malfunction in the cubicles' control system, illusion and reality could merge. Their wonderful travel facility worked because of a quantum anomaly even they didn't totally understand. However unlikely, the chance of being trapped in a dimension riven with wars and lacking outside toilets was enough to fill the antiseptic, adult mind with dread. The 12-year-old Suki still had an outlook open enough to trust illusion. Other young people just wallowed in the wonder of it all.

The children entering the cubicle next to hers were about to enter the ultimate dentists' nightmare, Sugar Candy Land. They weren't bothered by their parents' irrational anxiety that they would be swallowed by a giant marshmallow or carried off by a marzipan magpie. Nat, aged eight, was careful to keep the control box out of his four-year-old sister's reach. Temptation should have been Angelina's middle name.

Suki closed the door of her cubicle and watched its monitor count towards the supposed date of the Cretaceous chocolate sea. Then she paused the program to slowly edge it forwards until the world on the other side of the cubicle screen came into focus. As soon as the scene resolved itself the safety shutter rolled back. Suki stepped through the screen into a prehistoric valley filled with cycads and ferns.

As she walked towards a volcano it was like entering the hatchery of her uncle's ancient chicken farm, only not many of the creatures here chirped in quite the same manner. There was just the grinding of gizzard stones and munching of huge molars.

Suki felt the footsteps of something massive shake the ground. However safe the system was supposed to be, she still glanced about nervously to make sure she wasn't being hunted by a Tyrannosaurus rex. She was surrounded by nothing more aggressive than a herd of herbivorous hadrosaurs.

The time and location on her control box was correct, but there was no chocolate to be seen anywhere. The old mineral analyser must have been faulty. It was a family heirloom made in 2050, long before Suki had been born. Some palaeontologists claimed these models were the most reliable ever produced; now she could prove them wrong.

In their world of candyfloss clouds, marzipan flowers and toffee trees, Nat and Angelina were blissfully unaware of the dinosaurs in the travel cubicle next door. The sight of castles sculpted in iced coconut and surrounded by lemonade moats was enough to rot the teeth of any adult. To Angelina's sweet tooth it all made glorious sense. Nat wasn't quite so sure. His maturing taste buds now preferred the savoury, and he had actually started to like broad beans and broccoli. This was the last time he wanted to experience Sugar Candy Land. Soon he would be old enough to just eat the cake and leave the icing.

Nat dawdled after Angelina as she skipped through fronds of liquorice ferns, only stopping to insist that he instruct the control box to conjure up macaroon mountains and lakes of golden syrup. To keep her happy, Nat obliged, wondering how much it would take to overload the system controlling the travel cubicles. The control box's needle was dangerously near the red side of the dial, and he really didn't want to find out. But Angelina next bullied him into calling up a pineapple pizza over an acre wide. The needle began to tremble towards DANGER. Immediately after that she demanded a hill of peach ice cream to slide down.

Nat decided that this was enough. "Give it a rest, can't you! Sit down for a moment and be quiet!"

Angelina pouted petulantly, but her brother held the control and she had no choice but to sulkily obey. Nat leaned back on a cushion of Turkish delight and foolishly closed his eyes to bask in the sickly rays of the marzipan sun. This was all the opportunity Angelina needed to understand how the control box worked. It was simple; she just needed to tap out the letters of the item she wanted and, above it, how many and how large. Like most four-year-olds, Angelina knew how to spell chocolate.

Unfortunately, she wasn't so good at arithmetic.

23

Suki climbed the pumice slope of the volcano to look out over the landscape. The hadrosaurs were still browsing on the ferns and cycads. None of them seemed to be craving anything sweeter.

Then the ground shook. For a cold, clammy second Suki thought that the volcano was going to erupt.

The screen on her control box was flashing. The system controlling the travel cubicles was going into overload. If Suki didn't get out of the holographic program before illusion and reality merged she would be trapped in this prehistoric world forever.

The portal was on the other side of the valley. Suki ran for her life back down the volcano.

Nat was woken suddenly by a horrible sense of foreboding. "What the..?"

He found himself surrounded by towering cliffs of hazelnut chocolate. The needle on the control box was vibrating at "danger" and Angelina was looking suspiciously angelic.

Somewhere, deep below them, the travel cubicle matrix was about to explode.

Suki hurtled down the volcano's slope as the distant mountains started to melt in the fierce heat.

Her prehistoric program had merged with the one in the next cubicle. Surprised hadrosaurs found themselves crunching barley sugar branches and marzipan leaves, passing triceratops' horns were caught up in the caramel twigs of pear drop trees, and pterodactyls' wings became stuck in candyfloss clouds.

Two children were dashing towards Suki. They were shrieking at the tops of their voices as they tried to outrun a tide of liquid chocolate.

Suki's path to the portal was now cut off by the hot brown river and she only just managed to catch the children and pull them back up the volcano's pumice slope.

"Why didn't the safety cut-out cancel the programs?!" Nat almost screamed, unable to comprehend what had happened.

Angelina was too guilty to panic. What she did really couldn't have been that terrible. She looked sheepishly at the waves of chocolate licking the slope. "What does 'ten hazelnut chocolate bars to the power of 1000' mean?"

As though to confirm her question, huge lumps began to rise to the chocolate's surface. They weren't only going to drown, they were going to be pulverised by giant hazelnuts as well.

Suki noticed Nat's control box. The instructions, 'Ten hazelnut chocolate bars to the power of 1000', were still on its display.

She gulped. "You didn't - did you?"

"That is how you spell chocolate, isn't it?" asked the four-year-old.

"No, that's how you spell DISASTER!"

Nat's panic had turned to fury. "If we ever get out of here I'm going to nail your teddy bear to the helicar's garage and use it for laser practise!" he bellowed at his sister.

Angelina burst into tears.

A thick brown wave lifted the slab of pumice the young people had crowded onto and set them adrift on a sea of chocolate. Suki seized a barley sugar branch and tried to guide them towards the portal entrance.

Angelina stopped bawling.

Nat took his fingers out of his ears. "But surely... if this is only an illusion, we can't come to any harm - can we?"

25

Suki said nothing. If the rock sample she had discovered was authentic, then so was the sea of chocolate and hazelnuts under their pumice raft.

The children passed the worried looking hadrosaurs that had huddled on high ground above the lapping waves. Would being fossilised in hot chocolate be any better than falling into a bubbling pitch bog?

As soon as Suki, Nat and Angelina had almost reached the portal entrance, the three ton dinosaurs decided to plunge into the chocolate sea and start to swim.

Large waves picked up the pumice raft and spun it round and round.

Suddenly they were catapulted into the air. The marzipan sun began to dribble down the blue icing sky, giant chocolate hadrosaurs were swimming through a tide of custard, and the volcano erupted hazelnuts.

Dizzy and bruised, Suki, Nat, and Angelina found themselves on a platform pulsating with mauve light and surrounded by figures in protective clothing.

"Well congratulations kids!" announced a gruff voice, "You're still alive, though I can't think why!"

Suki was still dazed. "What happened?"

The woman with the gruff voice removed her visor. "You've managed to rewrite history."

Nat looked terrified. "How?"

"Instead of the dinosaurs being wiped out by a comet, they lost all their teeth through eating nothing but chocolate."

Angelina wanted to ask why they didn't get false ones, but she hadn't seen anyone with such a fierce expression since trying to make toffee in her father's cut glass trophy for airbeam racing.

Suki was bolder. "But chocolate must have some nutritional value, and it had to drain away eventually."

"It did, but how do you chew palm fronds and cycad nuts without any teeth!" The stern woman turned to Angelina. "And you are banned until you learn simple arithmetic!"

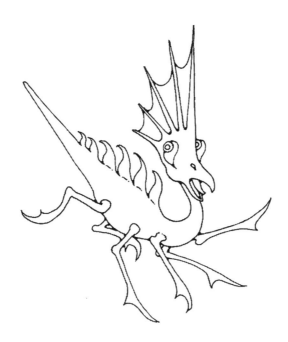

THE JUGLE EGG

The desert floor would soon be hot enough to bake a protein biscuit.

Alisia pulled on her wooden soled shoes and looked out over the dull, brown sandscape studded with thornbushes and the odd brilliant flower. Something nearby chirped in alarm and scuttled away. As the rays of the second sun struck Fire Mountain the desert seemed to blaze.

Alisia pulled on her hood and cloak to protect her from the ultra violet radiation then started to walk.

Her scanner whirred as it pinpointed the location of the others in the search party. Most of them were too old and slow to keep up with Alisia, and hoping they wouldn't need to spend another night in the desert. Their old, crashed spaceship in the shelter of a plateau was far more comfortable. Its water recycling system had long since failed, but they had a nearby well and solar panels to operate a pump. Their diet of water and protein biscuits may have been well-balanced, yet was boring beyond belief. Most of the stranded group would have walked to the other side of the huge desert if they thought there was any chance of finding fresh fruit there.

Unfortunately this planet's crust wasn't stable and the crew had spent years hoping a rescue party would arrive before their settlement was swallowed by an earthquake.

Alisia had not known any other home and was used to the parched world. She was fascinated by the strange reason her parents had ended up there. It all seemed too fantastic, even for an 11-year-old imagination. Perhaps they had invented the story to keep her amused, or decades of exposure to the two suns, twenty moons, and relentless heat had turned their Earthly brains.

Most of the science crew seemed crazy anyway, as they experimented with their cracked instruments, took peculiar readings from monitoring systems and scanned for the slightest anomaly on the small world. There were plenty of lizard-like creatures and insects the size of toads, yet the scientists were searching for something much larger, something that should have appeared well before Alisia was born. When they believed an anomaly worth investigation had been detected, every spare member of the crew was sent out to investigate.

As Alisia trudged on there were rumblings from deep in the ground. Somewhere in the mantle the planet's crust was about to throw a tantrum. There was a beep from her scanner. It warned Alisia she was entering the region of dimensional fluctuation.

Could it be? Had this mysterious anomaly actually arrived at last?

Without warning, Alisia was flattened to the ground by the downbeat of huge wings. When she looked up the creature had gone. Was this really supposed to happen? On Earth there was the legend that the Phoenix rose anew from the ashes of the fire with which it had immolated itself. Here, the Jugle was supposed to lay an egg that hatched the gateway to another dimension through which it could be reborn. Alisia had never believed in the legend and thought that the mission had just been sent to find the mysterious civilisation that did. If they had ever existed, their artefacts were now buried metres below the sand of this benighted planet.

The excited search party were dashing towards Alisia. She rearranged her UV cloak and looked down at a fresh crater in the desert floor. In its centre a huge egg pulsed with light. Alisia was now convinced that the mythical Jugle bird existed, and probably the people who believed in it; for all the good it had done them.

The egg was huge.

"They'll never move it", she laughed to herself, though wasn't sure why that should be funny, especially when there was another rumble deep in the planet's crust. It looked as though it was going to be academic anyway. The desert would be the only safe place until the quakes were over.

So the space ship under the shelter of its unstable plateau was quickly evacuated. Soon, In the dim light of the setting red sun the crew was camped round the crater where the egg sat. Scientists monitored its every vibration while the others watched and listened apprehensively as the shaking of the planet's crust increased.

Then the small planet gave a convulsive shudder.

In the distance their spaceship tipped skywards and was swallowed into a huge fissure that opened at the base of the plateau. They were now stranded without water in a desert that would turn into a furnace as soon as the intense second sun rose.

The adults said nothing, just sat and watched the alien egg.

As the tremors increased and the lightning rent the night sky the egg became translucent. Inside it a tangle of excited molecules pushed the shell out as though it were a huge bud trying to burst into flower. The egg grew larger and larger until it filled the crater like a dome. Inside was a dimension filled with light.

Alisia stood on the rim and stared at the world forming below them. There were valleys, waterfalls, lacy clouds, and flower filled meadows. And in the far distance, a gleaming city hung in the crystal, cobalt sky like a cloud of sequins.

She turned back to see the plateau crumbling into the fissure after their spaceship. The adults didn't move, either transfixed by the spectacle, or not daring to.

There was nothing else for it. Alisia jumped from the crater rim, through the thin wall of the translucent dome, and into another dimension.

Alarmed, her mother immediately followed. Then, one by one, the rest of the crew, until everyone found themselves standing in a flower filled meadow. Below them a beautiful alien world stretched away into the distance.

Then they looked back. On the other side of the dome was the dusty desert riven by earthquakes and lightning. Before anyone could have an irrational impulse to dart back to collect a piece of valuable equipment or protein biscuits, something invisible unfurled huge wings and flattened them to the ground with the draught from their downbeat.

When they got up the desert had vanished. They were on a new world.

Alisia looked at the intense blue sky and realised that they were galaxies away from anything she was familiar with. But she didn't mind. They were now, at last, going to meet the ancient civilisation who had also escaped to this magical planet.

THE ODD FISH

First published by Aquila in August 1994

Angela had never seen so many teeth on a fish. But then, it was a very odd fish. Its body had several ridges running from snout to tail like a reinforced box, its scales were large and leathery, and it was in a very bad mood. It had been trapped in a rock pool as the tide went out and in fury its powerful tail was whisking away the water that remained.

"Don't do that," Angela told it, "you'll make all the water run out, then you'll suffocate."

The fish peered at Angela with round red eyes as though it wanted her for breakfast.

"Just how long have you been stuck like that?" Angela asked.

After a long pause the fish opened its fierce jaws and said. "If you are so worried about it, why don't you carry me out to sea?"

Angela looked at its sharp teeth. "Goodness no, you might bite."

"And make you drop me? I may be a fish, but I am not stupid."

33

Its fins were very sturdy, like convenient handles, so Angela picked it up.

As she walked with it towards the outgoing sea she asked the fish, "What were you doing so close to the cliff and all those rocks?"

"That's where I used to live."

"What? In the rocks?"

"Oh yes."

"That's silly. Nothing could live in those rocks. There's nothing to eat."

Despite being out of water for some minutes, the fish wasn't gasping for breath. When Angela put it down in the shallow swell it looked up at her, balancing on its powerful fins like an irritable footstool.

"You are a very odd fish," insisted Angela.

"Perhaps I am," it replied, then turned and waddled into the sea.

In the distance Angela's mother was waving to her so she ran back up the beach. Angela's brother had built a large, ugly sand castle and her father had fallen asleep in a deckchair.

"Mum..."

Angela's mother stopped knitting and looked at her daughter.

"Shouldn't fish be soft and slippery?"

"Of course."

"Not hard, like a bike saddle with two rows of sharp teeth?"

Angela's mother was puzzled. "Not usually. What makes you ask?"

"Oh, nothing. Can I go and play by those rocks over there?"

"Yes, so long as you don't climb up them."

Angela went round every rock she could reach, searching for the home of the odd fish. Where had it come from? How had it managed to breathe when the tide went out? She was about to give up her search when, at last, in one of the large rocks, she found a shallow depression shaped just like her fish. In the impression she could count its teeth and tough scales.

Angela insisted her mother come and look at it. She became very excited and phoned the local museum. Within an hour a young woman with a small pick and a large satchel arrived. When she saw the impression of the fish in the rock she was even more excited.

The next day a group of people came from London. Angela was allowed to watch as they measured, sketched and took photos of the fish, which they called a fossil. Then the fossil hunters started to search the other rocks and shingle. The young woman from the museum told Angela that there ought to be another part to the fossil, the part which had made the impression in the rock.

"Are you sure that there was nothing else like this near here?" a bearded, middle-aged man asked Angela.

"Only the fish," said Angela.

"The fish?" The man's eyes lit up.

"But it swam away."

"But it couldn't have swum away." The man sounded puzzled. "It would have been millions of years old and made of stone."

"I thought it seemed odd," said Angela.

"Odd?"

"Yes. I suppose I should have known it wasn't a real fish by the way it talked."

The man's eyebrows furrowed and he shook his head. Angela knew then that the odd fish would have to remain her own special secret.

QUEENIE

David watched the rivulet of water wend its way down the dirty window pane. What had made him want to do his homework in the boathouse today of all days? It was cold, wet, and almost tea time.

He was about to pack his knapsack and wander home when there was a splash. He turned back to see a plump rat struggling in the water.

A rat! David hated them even more than snakes. And rats were supposed to be excellent swimmers. Where was the point in them leaving a sinking ship in the middle of some ocean if they weren't? But he couldn't stand there and watch this one drown.

David pushed an oar into the water so the rat could scurry to safety. As it landed on the planking of the small dock, he leapt back just in case it wanted to thank him. A brief squeak and disappearing tail would have been quite sufficient. Unfortunately the large, plump rat was tame and better mannered. It sat in its haunches and gazed up enquiringly at its rescuer. The resident rats had probably pushed it in the water for being too cute.

Having come to some decision, the rodent went to the boathouse entrance where it turned and squeaked urgently at David. He sighed. Which would be more fun, going home to finish his homework on the causes of the French Revolution or chasing a plump rat through the pouring rain? Then he realised that it had stopped raining and the sun was now valiantly trying to break through.

So David followed the rat outside. He locked the boathouse door and slipped the key through the park gatehouse's letter box as he passed.

Instead of returning to civilisation and its worried owner, the plump rat headed for a narrow path which led into the bramble wood.

36

"No way!" David told it. His track suit was too new to run through rampant thorns.

The rat stopped. It sat on its haunches and cast him a look of contempt.

"That only leads to the old air raid shelter." The rodent's gaze was unwavering. "Oh, all right, but this had better be good." He just hoped that no one was eavesdropping.

The rat scampered off.

His track suit soon drenched and snagged, David doggedly pursued the intermittent flash of white and brown bouncing through the bracken, past the air raid shelter, and down to the river.

Peering from holes in the bank were dozens of small, inquisitive faces. To some people, like his immature sister, this would have been pure Disney. To David, it was a job for the Pied Piper of Hamlin. What on Earth had he expected to find after following a fancy rat, other than its huge family of multi coloured rodents?

David sat on a fallen tree trunk to examine the damage to his snagged track suit sodden with mud. It had been a present from his parents and he was going to be in deep trouble somewhere between the back door and the washing machine. He tried to pull some of the snags through to the other side. It only made matters worse, so he turned his attention to the rodents.

Where had so many pet rats come from? Then had to admit that he really wasn't too bothered.

Wet and irritated, David decided to go home. As soon as he got up the plump rat darted ahead, squeaking urgently to get him to follow it again. At least this route was free of brambles, mud, and wet overhanging branches so David trudged after the rodent.

He followed it out of the wood and across a road to a track leading to a bland, brick building. David hesitated. This was spooky. His parents trusted him to be careful, and he could outrun anyone. However, what did you do when tempted to enter a bleak building in cthe middle of nowhere?

The door was ajar and inside was lit by harsh, fluorescent light. On a long bench were rows of cages, their doors open.

"Oh no!" David gasped. "Animal research."

Now shaking, he reluctantly followed the plump rat to a door at the far end of the corridor. It was locked.

The rat climbed onto the bench and squeaked at a hook hidden behind a cage. On it was a key.

David took it down and unlocked the door.

The room was dark so he fumbled about the door frame until he found a light switch. As soon as he pressed it everything was flooded with a lurid glow. Didn't red lights mean vampires and getting run over by cars that jumped them?

Forcing himself not to dash back out, David went to the Perspex cage in the middle of the room. Inside it was a large bundle of fur.

There was the wailing of sirens in the distance and the creature lifted its head.

"Well," a voice squeaked, "either open the cage door, or run away before you're caught."

The sirens were getting closer and, without thinking, David opened the cage and lifted out - he wasn't sure what.

Before he could reach the main door, a young woman in a white overall blocked his way. David tried to hide the creature in his track suit top.

"Do you mind," it complained. "How would you like to be pushed into someone's damp jacket?"

Then David realised where the squeaky voice was coming from. "Urrk!"

The young woman raised a hand. "It's all right."

Through the open door he could see military vehicles pulling up. The men leaping out of them had guns. To David, things looked far from all right.

"This way!" The young woman guided him down some steps in the floor. The plump rat followed and she bolted the trap door after them.

They ran along a damp tunnel for what seemed ages and eventually came out through the old air raid shelter in the wood.

The young woman pulled a whistle from her overall and gave a long blast on it. The other fancy rats immediately swarmed after them as they hurtled towards a car waiting near the gatehouse.

David was breathless by the time they reached it. "This is too weird," he gasped, and then looked down at the creature he was clutching. It was a large, very intelligent looking rodent the size of a cat.

"Meet Queenie," said the young woman.

David's jaw dropped. "Queenie? A talking rat? Who would want a talking rat?"

"The military. Could you think of a better way to spy on the enemy?"

No, David couldn't.

She took Queenie from David. "Sorry, got to go. You'd better make yourself scarce as well." Then she opened the car door. The rats swarmed into it.

With a brief wave the young woman drove off, Queenie sitting on her lap.

Army searching the area or not, David was unable to move for some while.

He was still there when Mr and Mrs Holt returned to the park gatehouse after doing the weekly shopping.

"Hi David," Mrs Holt called as she unloaded bags from the boot of their car. "You look as though you've been jogging through the brambles."

"Yeah," groaned David. "Me mum's going to kill me."

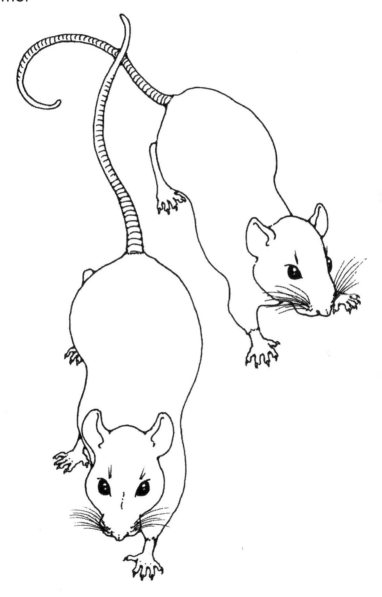

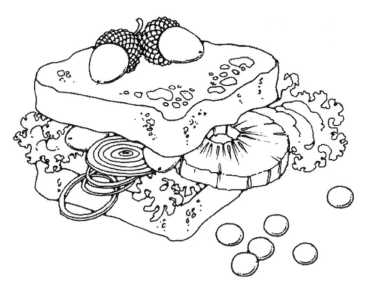

SAMMY'S SANDWICH

Melissa turned up her pointed nose and sneered as though someone had pushed a spadeful of manure under it. "Acorn and jam sandwiches?"

"No, marmalade," corrected Joel. "Acorn and marmalade… in a currant bun."

"What person with normal taste buds would eat acorns and jam in a currant bun?"

"Sammy does, though she much prefers raw mushrooms and honey in Rivita. She used to like vinegar on them as well, but it made them soggy," explained Joel. "She's got these amazing teeth and likes to bite into things."

David was beginning to lose his appetite for the dinner of grilled sausages waiting for him at home. "Yuk! Where did you find this character? Sitting on a toadstool?"

Joel smiled agreeably. "No, actually she was sitting on the old mayor's tomb - You know, the one with the Victorian angels." It was no good; he knew the expression his friends wore all too well. "You don't want to come and meet her then?"

"I'm playing tennis with Angela," said Melissa hastily.

David also backed away. "Me Mum will wonder where I am."

Joel shrugged and grinned to himself as they scurried off. Melissa was a snob, and David scared of his own shadow.

Joel pushed his hands into his pockets and sauntered off towards St Minion's, the parish church, and wondered how Sammy would like the sandwich he had in his satchel. This time he had excelled himself. His parents were going to wonder about the amount of mustard he had used, though they surely wouldn't miss that slice of elderly pineapple and crusts from yesterday's loaf.

Joel picked a few sprigs of hawthorn and half ripe sloes. There were several ancient yew trees in the graveyard and Sammy was crazy enough to try a handful of their berries for dessert instead. As they got on so well, he didn't want their friendship to end abruptly.

There she was in the late afternoon sun, sitting cross legged on the corn merchant's tomb.

Joel joined Sammy and pulled out the pungent brown paper bag containing her sandwich. As his friend smelt the fragrant meal her eyebrows arched in approval, and in four gulps it was gone.

The friends chatted about dragons, food, and boys who wear Bermuda shorts, and then Joel pointed to the hardly legible inscription below them. "Tell me about the corn merchant?"

Sammy chewed a few bitter sloe berries before remembering, "Oh yes, his family built a watermill. The local miller was afraid of losing business so paid some locals to divert the course of the stream one night." Sammy gave a grin so wide she resembled a frog.

42

"What happened?"

"The stream flooded several orchards and destroyed the trees, so the farmers burnt down his windmill."

"Then what happened?"

"Black Death arrived the next day. They all died." Sammy pointed to several medieval gravestones. "Everyone."

The sun was setting and painting everything with its long red rays.

Joel shuddered. "I'd better go now, Sammy. Will you be here next week?"

"As long as there's no weddings or funerals. They don't like me being down here when there's weddings and funerals."

Joel jumped down from the tomb. "Have you ever tried pitta bread?"

Sammy scratched her flat nose. "Filled with those nice crunchy corn bits and onion?"

"Cornflakes and onion?" Joel shrugged. "If you like." He fastened his satchel and put the smelly brown paper bag which had contained Sammy's sandwich in the graveyard waste bin. "See you next week then."

Sammy wistfully watched him go.

As the sun set, two granite wings unfurled with a sharp crack from her short back. A brisk downbeat propelled her upwards to the corner of the 60 foot high bell tower where she precariously perched, overlooking the small parish. Slivers of quartz glinted in Sammy's eyes as her smile became stony, and a water spout appeared between her lips.

The pride of St Minion's, the church's last intact gargoyle, glowed as she caught the last rays of the descending sun.

TIGGER, TREACLE AND COKE

The dream was back.

However hard he tried to wake up, Looda was yet again caught up in its nonsensical talons.

Round and round a strange garden the two children chased Looda until he was exhausted. Then when they caught him, it was his turn to chase them. Why couldn't Treacle and Coke spend their time sitting in front of a screen like most other children? This sort of thing was too exhausting to be good for anyone.

Next Looda was dragged to the plastic seesaw and bounced up and down until it cracked. It was a reverberating sound and someone must have noticed. Undaunted, Treacle and Coke pulled him away to play on the swings.

By the time the children stopped for breath, Looda was so tired all he could do was lie down and stare at the goldfish in the pond. He must have been the only person who slept all night, only to wake up exhausted.

Looda had no idea why the nine-year-old girl was called Treacle, or her five-year-old brother, Coke. They insisted on calling him Tigger - Looda couldn't work that out either. It might have had something to do with the old striped fur coat of their grandmother's they insisted he wear when he had to gallop about the lawn, pulling them on a tricycle.

Neither Treacle nor Coke were allowed to climb the apple trees so, when he became too exhausted to play any more, Looda hid in their branches and watched the children wonder where he had gone. If he was totally honest with himself, he enjoyed his visits and the hectic play. Back home it was nothing but pay attention, and learn, learn, learn. There wasn't a word for play in his vocabulary; it was all about expanding the mind.

For some reason the brother and sister didn't have anyone else to play with, and their grandparents' garden was the only place they were allowed to let off steam. Treacle explained how she and Coke went to a special school. That was great fun, but it was for only a few hours a week. The rest of the time was very boring for the two boisterous young people. For someone whose life was filled with non stop, intensive study, Looda had trouble understanding what it was like. If only they could share out their play and study equally between the three of them, life would be so much easier.

Then Looda had an idea. He persuaded the boisterous Treacle and Coke to sit down while he told them everything he knew about the planets and stars. He wasn't sure if they understood, yet they insisted he told them more. So Looda went on to botany, geology, oceanography, meteorology, and biology - all the subjects he had passed with merit. The more his dream companions listened, the less tired he felt when he woke up.

Then Looda persuaded Treacle and Coke to try drawing. Not just the splashes and squirls they made at school, but things which could be recognised. The children's sketchpads were soon filled with beautiful, strange scenes, much to the amazement of their parents. After working all day, they seldom had the energy to be amazed at anything. And then they started to listen to the conversations Treacle and Coke were having. Despite the efforts of their teachers, the children had never shown much interest in any subject before. Now, between them, they were discussing things even the adults couldn't understand. Nor were they as rowdy as they used to be, and could even be trusted to load the dishwasher.

One morning, a teacher visited Treacle and Coke's grandparents.

Because they were now so well behaved, their grandmother had taken the children shopping, so their grandfather invited the young woman into the lounge. Her questions seemed endless and often pretty silly, but he was a good natured soul and knew they were being asked for the benefit of his grandchildren.

At last the teacher put away her clipboard, anxious to discuss the real reason she was there. "So what do you make of the children's rapid progress?"

Grandfather scratched his head. "They've always been nice kids; but have calmed down no end over these past few weeks."

"Any idea why?"

"Reckon it has something to do with that playmate of theirs."

"Playmate?"

"Oh yes; didn't we mention him? Small round feller. Always wears fancy dress for some reason. We always watch, but never interfere unless someone looks as though they're going to get hurt. Must be one of the neighbour's kids. Though, every time I go out to chat to him, he seems to disappear and the kids come over secretive. That's ok though. No one else comes round to play with them... them being the way they are... and they all get on like a house on fire, they do. Reckon he taught them how to draw."

The teacher peered over her glasses at the older man. "What sort of fancy dress does this child wear then?"

"Well, he always has on this glittery tunic, bit like purple baking foil . . . then there's these things on his head..."

"Things on his head?"

"Look like short stumpy horns. And, of course, the tail. Long and hairy it is. The way he swishes it about you'd swear it was real."

TWILLINGTON'S TIP

As soon as he saw the TWILLINGTON TOWN COUNCIL coat of arms Colin knew what the envelope contained. He opened the letter and read, feeling a pang of annoyance at the "Dear Master ..." After all, he was almost fourteen and at least warranted Mr. If they had addressed his friend Amy as "Miss" she would have set off stink bombs at every lamppost around the town hall, and she was only eleven. Amy was a "MS" in Doc Martins.

Perhaps Colin should have told her what he had been up to, but didn't like to admit that pacifism wasn't working.

The letter went on to condescendingly explain that Twillington created a lot of rubbish and it had to be dumped somewhere. So, where better than on the site of a derelict factory, safely tucked out of view from the gleaming new shopping centre with its smartly paved pedestrianised thoroughfares? The tip couldn't even be seen from the multi-storey car park so, "perhaps Master Colin Arnatt could suggest a better location?" Yes, Colin could. It involved demolishing the town hall while several council officers were still inside it.

The next time he stood on the hill overlooking the tip with Amy, he told her about his one boy campaign. She only laughed. Colin hardly expected her to do anything else. She always made him feel such a wimp when he tried to do the right thing.

Through the valley of rubbish below trickled an incongruously bright stream. It flowed on through Twillington, tastefully wending its way about the new shopping centre in a white stone conduit overhung by plants.

Feeling defeated, Colin moaned on about the vandalism of local government. Amy had stopped listening to him and was trying work out where the stream rose from. The shell of the Victorian factory was still standing and, hanging from an outer wall, were the rotting remains of a water wheel. The stream was now far too shallow to turn it. Further along the valley was a massive wall of brick and crumbling concrete in the hillside which looked as though it was trying to prevent the resident troll from bursting out.

Amy went down to the edge of the tip to pick up a sharp metal rod, and then strode off along the valley to the wall. Colin could tell by the determination in her stride that she had vandalism in mind. He dutifully bounded after her, wondering how she managed to negotiate the bricks littering the derelict factory site without snapping her ankles. It must have been the self defence classes.

The stench from the tip was overpowering enough to knock the scavenging gulls out of the sky. Holding a handkerchief over his nose as he went round the mounds of rotting rubbish, he climbed up the wall to reach Amy who was now standing on top of it.

Colin looked down at the stream as it trickled from an ancient pipe in the hillside. "Didn't know this is where the water came from? This wall must be sealing up an old tunnel. Could've been a railway track."

Amy pointed back to the derelict water wheel hanging from the old factory wall. "Or to work that."

"Canal?"

"Not enough water pressure." Amy prized away some bricks from the wall and they tumbled into the detritus filling the gully below.

Several rats scurried for cover.

"Don't do that! It can't be safe as it is."

Knowing Colin was more worried by rats than a few stray bricks, Amy turned her attention to the hillside. She randomly jabbed her metal probe into the ground. Small gushes of water flowed out.

"Jacob's Cave must be down there," Colin calculated. "My Dad showed me an entrance to it on the other side of this hill. He said that his great grandparents used to have picnics down there before it flooded. Every year their chapel arranged this outing for the congregation."

Amy watched the water trickling out of the hillside. "Need to wear flippers now."

Colin could tell by his friend's expression that she was plotting something he'd rather not know about.

"Let's go home now," he said firmly.

Amy continued to think. "You're really upset about this tip aren't you." It wasn't a question.

He answered it nevertheless. "Well of course I am. Look what's happened to the wildlife. There used to be voles and frogs and kestrels here only a couple of years ago, now there're only rats and seagulls, and that bad smell."

"Yeah, shame that," agreed Amy. "Let's go then."

Colin was too anxious to leave to wonder why she decided to do as he asked. Amy never did anything he asked. It was a point of honour. So he didn't turn round to see what she was doing and went back through the derelict factory and round the tip.

Sure that Colin was too far away to see what she was doing, Amy drove her metal spike deep into the crumbling bricks of the wall with several blows from a rock. Colin heard, but didn't want to know what she was up to. That way detention, severe reprimands, and nightmares lay.

"That should do it," Amy muttered to herself. She could calculate as well, albeit more instinctively.

As water started to push its way through the crack she had made in the wall she bounded after Colin.

He was relieved that she had decided to follow him after all and felt confident to ask when she caught up, "What did you just do?" without fear of a terrible answer.

"Just digging this out." Amy held up a piece of flint. "Could put a good edge on that."

"You know what your dad said he'd do if he caught you with anything sharp again so why bother to dig it out?"

"That concrete's almost eroded away."

"Then why make it worse?"

Amy laughed. "Come on, Mum says you're invited to our barbecue this evening. Bring that letter with you; she'll want to see it."

"Well, she's worried about green issues as well, isn't she," Colin gave his friend a stern glance, "unlike some people whose only interest in life is fried food."

Amy tossed the flint away. "Well excuse me for liking chip sandwiches."

It was almost midnight. Barbecue fumes still scented the air, and the new shopping centre was now empty as the last supermarket shutter came down.

Colin half woke at the sound of clattering, thought it was the washing machine, and went back to sleep, not awake enough to wonder why his father would be doing the laundry in the middle of the night.

A short while before the ancient brick wall on the hillside near the derelict factory had crumbled under the pressure of the water it held back. Those few bricks Amy had loosened became holes, then chasms...

Soon a torrent of water poured into the valley, slammed into the reeking tip and swept its contents through the town centre. No longer contained by the polished stone conduit that had guided it on its tasteful way, the river picked up vehicles in the lower levels of the car park and clattered them against each other. The wall of water continued to push the rancid rubbish through the gleaming shopping centre and into the main street where it deposited much of its load on the steps of Twillington Town Hall, as well as flooding the basement from where council tax demands were issued.

A lone security guard and his dog had to run too hard to call for help. When reinforcements eventually did arrive, all the fire service could do was watch the town's garbage slop against their water tenders and corporation flower tubs and litter bins bob about like corks in the filthy water.

Then came the rats.

In sinuous formation, they swarmed from the water and up drainpipes, into gutters, lofts, offices, shops, and even banks. The council's pest control officer couldn't cope and had to call in private experts to help evict them.

Having found its natural level, the river that once drove a Victorian factory water wheel lay contentedly on its reclaimed flood plain, the detritus on its surface alive with flies. It couldn't seep away because the ground had been concreted over.

Amongst the letters stored in the town hall's basement, one mockingly floated on the water's surface.

It began,

"Dear Sir or Madam,

I would respectfully like to draw your attention the damage caused to the environment by the new council tip..."

ZALDA ZAX AND THE CYBERPOD

"Now," said Mr Knox, "I want at least three pages on 'Frankenstein' by tomorrow morning."

Kevin sharpened his pencil and started to write.

"Not now, you stupid boy. It's lunch hour."

The break bell was muffled by the sound of trainers stampeding to the canteen for curry and chips and the click of the English teacher's shoes as he followed them.

Kevin carried on writing. 'Zalda Zax guided her spaceship through the opening shutter. On the other side of the bulkhead was the machine that controlled the moon's orbit. After working perfectly for years, it had now gone wrong. But it had its own defence system against terrorists and might not recognise that the engineer had come to mend it...'

Unfortunately, at that point, Mr Knox returned to the classroom, possibly because he had forgotten something, but more likely to catch Kevin out. This was a man who needed someone smaller to humiliate, and Kevin seldom failed to give him a reason. The teacher snatched up the page and read it before Kevin could conceal his story.

"You stupid boy," he sighed pityingly. "When will you learn to grow up? If you want to survive in this world you'll need both feet on the ground."

Kevin said nothing. He suspected that Mr Knox's parents had nailed his shoes to the floor before he was tall enough to reach for the biscuit tin.

The English teacher snatched up a folder from his desk and swept out like a majestic tug battling the oncoming waves of pupil ignorance.

Kevin looked despondently at his story, roughly folded the page, and pushed it into his pocket.

All through cookery, while making pancakes, thoughts of the defective moon machine bounced back into Kevin's bored mind. Why couldn't he be gluten intolerant like Tyrone, and allowed to sit the period out in the library? To make matters worse, the class now had to make fudge for mother's day.

Kevin surreptitiously took the crumpled page from his pocket, laid it on a pastry board and began to scribble under the cover of a large saucepan of bubbling sugar. 'The machine had been put at the centre of the moon to stabilise its orbit round the Earth after being struck by a comet. Without the moon the Earth's orbit could become so irregular no one would survive the change in climate. Zalda Zax was the only one who could get through its defences to find out why the moon was being pulled towards the Earth. The gyroscope must have been sabotaged...'

There was a sharp, sweet smell of burning sugar. Kevin's fudge was now caramelised. He took the saucepan to the sink and filled it with water. When the teacher was able to see through the steam, she scowled and went back to her star pupil who had graduated to making a mushroom soufflé.

Kevin shook the flour from his story and wondered if he ought to forget about Zalda Zax and the moon machine and take an interest in reality, but the idea of the space woman was very persistent.

With a box of pancakes brittle enough to use as frisbees and bag of burnt fudge tucked under his arm, Kevin meandered home. He had to cross the park before it was dark or his mother would worry.

Kevin was passing the fence of the infants' playground when he felt as though he had just walked through a patch of rather stiff air. Then everything became unnervingly quiet. Even the traffic on the nearby main road seemed miles away. The playground was still there, yet on the other side of it he could see spinning lights, and they certainly didn't belong to the traffic roundabout.

Kevin watched in frightened curiousity as he realised that the lights came from an odd craft. Its shape kept changing, as though spheres were rotating inside larger spheres. Then it materialised. Common sense told Kevin to run for his life; fascination insisted he would never forgive himself if he did.

A short figure was a silhouetted against a circle of intense light. Kevin's optic nerves were numbed. It was unlikely fairies were able to plug into the National Grid, so the creature had to be an alien.

For Kevin, reality and fantasy could sometimes merge. His parents despaired of him ever telling them apart. And now the problem seemed to be rearing its ugly head yet again.

The visitor came towards him. She wore a helmet more like an Olympic skier's than an astronaut's and a gold suit, over which was a short waistcoat with pockets full of tools he didn't recognize.

There was an embarrassed silence as Kevin gawped and the astronaut gleamed.

"Hi," said Kevin, raising a limp hand. "How's things?"

It was an idiotic thing to come out with under the circumstances, but it encouraged the strange visitor to remove her helmet and reveal a sixteen-year-old human.

She raised a golden glove. "Hi. You called Kevin?"

Kevin gulped. "That's me." There were a million Kevins so she must have got the wrong one. "What're you doing here?"

"I need that story you were writing."

Perhaps she had found the right Kevin after all. They couldn't all be as nerdy as him.

"You what?"

"Your story about the moon machine."

Kevin pulled the crumpled page from his pocket. "You mean this? But how did you know about it?"

"My name is Zalda Zax."

Kevin looked at the golden suited visitor in amazement. "But you can't be Zalda Zax. I thought you up."

"You gave that story to an ancestor of mine. I was named after the character you created."

"I don't understand? Why is this story so important?" Kevin tried to flatten the crumpled page on the Tupperware box containing his pancakes.

"You gave my ancestor the idea which will eventually destroy the Earth."

Kevin gasped. "Then ... you must be a time traveller? But I don't know anyone who could be your ancestor?" He held up his story. "And I haven't given this to anyone. I never give anyone my stories. They always laugh at them. And it's not really finished."

"It doesn't matter. It's the idea that persuaded my ancestor to create the moon machine."

"You mean this ancestor really does go on to make a device that can alter the moon's orbit?"

"Right, and that's why you're coming with me to see why you shouldn't put the idea into her head."

"Wouldn't that mean interfering with time? I mean... Doctor Who wouldn't allow me to do that."

"What has your doctor got to do with this?"

Kevin became agitated. "But you can't alter history! It's wrong!"

"After you see what happened, you'll change your mind."

Kevin didn't remember boarding the timeship. It just somehow surrounded him.

"I'll be late for tea," he protested weakly. He was more in awe of his mother than extraterrestrial excursions.

Zalda Zax was too busy with the controls of the ship to pay much attention. "No you won't. You can be back at exactly the same time. Why not eat your pancakes if you're afraid of missing your tea?"

Kevin wasn't that hungry.

"Fasten your safety belt."

Without warning they entered a vortex in space where time and gravity ceased to exist. Kevin's tongue was paralysed, so he was compelled to listen to the time traveller.

"In your lifetime, the orbit of the moon becomes irregular. It affects the Earth's orbit and rotation. We now know it would have corrected itself, but people were alarmed by the change in the weather and earthquakes it caused. My ancestor invented a machine that could stabilise the orbit of a moon by increasing its atomic mass. Her original idea had been to adjust the moons of Mars so it could be made habitable for the world's huge population. That would have taken centuries, but back then it was more important to stabilise our moon's orbit."

"So what happened?"

"The machine was sabotaged and the moon came too close to the Earth. The resulting tides washed away a large proportion of the human race - mostly those who didn't have credit cards."

At last they came out of the time tunnel and Kevin was able to think again. He pulled a clean sheet of paper from his duffle bag and started to write, using his Tupperware box of pancakes as a desk.

"What are you doing?" asked Zalda.

"Frankenstein."

"Frankenstein?"

"I have to do this homework for Fort Knox by tomorrow morning," lied Kevin.

The time traveller gave him an unsure glance, and then guided the ship down to show him a devastated Earth. Large areas were still flooded. The surviving population were further inland, rebuilding their cities.

Kevin continued to write.

Zalda was exasperated. "What are you doing?"

"Changing history."

"What do you mean?"

Kevin had erased the original story about the moon machine. "I'm changing the plot. Hang onto your space socks - just in case." After writing two more sentences Kevin looked up. "How about this: - 'Zalda Zax switched the controls of her ship to light drive. The cyberpod, the monster machine invented by her distant ancestor, must have thought she had escaped.'"

"No!" protested Zalda. "That's even worse!"

"Wait," shushed Kevin. "Not finished; 'The cyberpod had originally been invented as a welding machine. Instead of heat, it used sound waves so powerful it could join together girders heavy enough to support ten Eiffel Towers. But now it was out of control.'"

"What are you trying to do, you stupid boy?!"

Before Kevin could explain, time blinked. They were suddenly light years away from the Earth. Zalda's timeship was much larger and her pressure suit was blue instead of gold.

Below them, illuminated by a giant red sun, was a round machine with hundreds of hinged appendages like legs. It was peering up at the timeship like a spider waiting to pounce. A couple of silver legs rotated as though lining up a weapons system.

"What the ...?" Changing Zalda's identity so dramatically hadn't helped her presence of mind.

"Alright?" Kevin asked innocently.

She shook her head as her mind adapted to its new persona. "Yes ... Of course. Must have been the time hop." Now totally accepting the situation, Zalda looked down at the cyberpod. "That thing's arming itself."

Kevin felt smug. "It's all right, it uses sound waves so can't do any harm until it's in an atmosphere."

Zalda Zax was not impressed. "Stupid boy, why did I bring you with me?"

"Long story. You may not believe it." Kevin hesitated. "But sound waves can't travel through space," he insisted.

"They can't, but its laser beam can."

A beam of light sliced through the ship.

Alarms wailed and automatic extinguishers filled the cockpit with fine powder.

Kevin quickly fastened his safety belt. "Why wasn't the hull depressurised?"

"It's a time ship."

Kevin was an avid Doctor Who fan, yet didn't for one second believe that the way the Tardis hopped time had anything to do with reality. "What's the difference?"

"You don't know much, do you."

Totally deflated, Kevin listened as Zalda explained the universe created by his inspired helpfulness.

In this dimension the cyberpod had laid waste to several mining planets in its search for minerals to weld, cutting through bulkheads and compelling the miners to escape up emergency shafts to the surface. From there they watched as their hard won ore was smelted and welded into mountainous works of art. They were so monstrous the sight of them would have sent any life-form with a sense of proportion into shock.

"Oh well," Kevin muttered, "better than the Earth drowning I suppose."

Zalda looked up from programming repairs. "What was that?"

"Nothing. Just wondering how long this cyberpod's been on the rampage?"

"Long enough to give metal sculptors a bad name."

"I mean, it hasn't actually killed anyone, has it?" Kevin asked anxiously.

"The only casualties so far have been a few art lovers who had seizures."

"What are you going to do about it?"

"Send it to art classes."

"No, really?"

"Switch the thing off - with a missile. What else?" Zalda opened Kevin's box of brittle pancakes and broke a piece from one.

Kevin knew it would give her indigestion. "Can't you reprogram the thing?"

She stopped crunching. "How?"

"Doesn't it have a remote control unit somewhere..? " Kevin foundered; he hadn't had time to write one into the story before the plot gained this dangerous momentum of its own.

"Yes," said Zalda, "and the cyberpod has hidden the thing where we can't find it." She helped herself to another pancake. "These are good."

Different dimension, different taste buds, thought Kevin, thankful he wasn't going to be blamed for upsetting her digestion.

"Its inventor must have had a spare system?"

Zalda looked amazed at his naivety. "This cyberpod is the 52nd model in the series and the only other remaining remote control unit is in some satellite museum of space research."

"Has anyone tried it?"

"You have got to be joking."

"Well, didn't you bring me along because I knew the inventor?"

Zalda bit thoughtfully into another pancake. "Well, yes."

"I know she wouldn't have designed a machine like that without a safety backup. I come from centuries before you and we could think of the obvious."

Having finished the pancakes, Zalda put aside the box and Kevin hoped she wouldn't notice the small bag of burnt fudge. It was unnerving to watch anyone eat his cooking, even if they did enjoy it.

Zalda tapped into the ship's memory. "All right. The museum's only four light years away."

Kevin didn't enjoy the sensation of his molecules parting company as they time hopped through space and, when the sixteen-year-old Zalda Zax told him she had actually been alive for two hundred years, he wasn't surprised. He just hoped he'd still be eleven if he ever got back home.

Despite the time hop, the cyberpod was still on their tail as they orbited the space museum satellite.

Zalda put the time ship slightly out of dimensional phase to baffle the cyberpod's scanners before it opened up with its laser in an attempt to remodel the ship into another tasteless sculpture. They would only be safe for a short time, so she took the beam lift down to the museum to see the curator.

Kevin watched as the cyberpod stalked round and round the ship like a huge boy-eating humbug, trying to focus on its target. Any movement would give the timeship's position away, so Kevin remained still. He felt as though felt he had been sitting there hours by the time Zalda returned with a plain grey box.

"That it then?"

"Well I didn't go down for the Traghartax's crown jewels." She opened the museum piece and tried tuning into several frequencies. "This had better work."

"It must."

There was a laser strike. The ship was now in phase and the cyberpod had sliced a piece out of its hull. Safety shutters whirred into place.

"Hurry up!" panicked Kevin. "Me Mum'll go mad if I don't get back home tonight."

"Oh shut-up," snapped Zalda, trying to concentrate.

After what felt like an eternity being buffeted by laser fire, the glowing shield that protected the cyberpod was lowered.

"You've done it! You've done it!" whooped Kevin. "Now you can reprogram it. You could get it to relandscape all the damage it's done."

"First, I'm going to program in some artistic sense."

Kevin didn't remember arriving back by the infants' playground. Zalda had probably sent him to sleep because he wouldn't shut-up. He must have imagined it all of course but, just in case, Kevin took the Zalda Zax story from his pocket and ripped it into small pieces, which he tossed into the nearest waste bin. It was then he realised that there were no pancakes rattling about in his Tupperware box. And the bag of caramelised fudge had disappeared.

For his homework on Frankenstein, Kevin rewrote the cyberpod story.

Mr Knox gave him two out of ten and a letter to take home for his mother.

Published by Dodo Books

www.dandi.me.uk/dodo/

Picture books by Dandi Palmer

An Odd Alphabet
The Grunnick
Angelo and the Sunbeam Jewel
Beaky and Squeaky
Possomly's Bomb
Ganesha, the Elephant-faced God
Mr Blot
Bumblechunk and Tangle-toof
The Sorcerer's Apprentice
Barnaby Bell's Hot Air Balloon
The Love for Three Oranges
King of Dolphin Island
Salvation and the Devil Dancer

Pictures to Colour In

***

Books for Older Children and Teenagers

The Glee Machine
Different Dragons
Green Fingers
Short Stories for Older,
and not quite so Old, Children

23346353R00043

Printed in Great Britain
by Amazon